994026

A BABY BORN IN
BETHLEHEM

MARTHA WHITMORE HICKMAN

illustrations by GIULIANO FERRI

ALBERT WHITMAN & COMPANY, MORTON GROVE, ILLINOIS

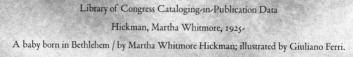

Library of Congress Cataloging-in-Publication Data

Hickman, Martha Whitmore, 1925-

A baby born in Bethlehem / by Martha Whitmore Hickman; illustrated by Giuliano Ferri.

p. cm.

Summary: Recounts the events surrounding the birth of Jesus, from the angel's announcement to Mary to the visit of the Wise Men in Bethlehem.

ISBN 0-8075-5522-3 (hc.)

1. Jesus Christ — Nativity — Juvenile literature. [1. Jesus Christ — Nativity. 2. Bible stories — N.T.] I. Ferri, Giuliano, ill. II. Title.

BT315.2.H53 1999

232.92 — dc21   98-54354

Text copyright © 1999 by Martha Whitmore Hickman.

Illustrations copyright © 1999 by Giuliano Ferri.

Published in 1999 by Albert Whitman & Company,

6340 Oakton, Morton Grove, Illinois 60053-2723.

Published simultaneously in Canada by

General Publishing, Limited, Toronto.

Printed in the United States of America.

10 9 8 7 6 5 4 3 2 1

The illustrations were done in watercolor and pencil.

The text type was set in Poliphilus.

The design is by Scott Piehl.

To Willie and Emma and Ben —M.W.H.

For my family —G.F.

ONE DAY LONG AGO, a young woman named Mary, who was engaged to a man named Joseph, was walking in her garden. Suddenly there appeared before her a beautiful angel.

"Mary!" the angel said, "I come to you from God!"

At first Mary was frightened, and she stepped back.

"Don't be afraid," the angel said. "God is pleased with you. God is going to make something wonderful happen to you."

"What could it be?" Mary asked, astonished.

"You will have a baby, a baby boy," the angel said. "His name will be Jesus. He will be called the Son of the Most High. And when he grows up, he will be king over all his people."

Then the angel went away. At first Mary sat quietly, thinking of what the angel had said. Then she stood up and danced her way out of the garden, and all that day she went around with singing in her heart.

So the weeks and months went by. Mary was happy. She and Joseph got ready for her baby.

But when it was almost time for the baby to be born, a ruling came from the emperor: all the people in the land must go to the town their families came from, to be registered for the census.

So Mary and Joseph set out for the town of Bethlehem, which was where their families were from. It was a long journey, up and down hills and across streams.

They walked, though sometimes Mary rode on their little donkey. The roads were crowded with other travelers, who, like them, were going to be registered.

By the time they reached Bethlehem, Mary was very tired. "We must find a place to stay," she said to Joseph. "I know this baby is coming soon."

Joseph began to look for a room. "Do you have a place for us, please?" he asked at every inn. "We are tired from our long journey, and Mary is about to have a baby. Do you have a room? Please?"

But all the rooms were filled with other travelers. "Sorry, try next door," one innkeeper after another told him. "Everything is taken. Sorry."

At last one kind man said, "I don't have any rooms left. But you can go to my stable. It's warm and dry. Would that do?"

"Oh, yes," Joseph said.

"Anything," Mary said, for she felt the baby was coming very soon now.

The innkeeper led them to the stable and went away. Mary sank back against the clean, sweet-smelling straw. She took Joseph's hand.

The donkey, tired from the journey, eagerly drank water from the basin. A dove flew in to sing on the ledge above where Mary lay. Tiny mice scurried around in excitement. A dog ran back and forth around the feet of the cows and oxen, who stood in the shadows shuffling their hooves and chewing hay.

And there, near the kindly animals, the Baby Jesus was born.

Mary wrapped him in swaddling clothes, which are bands of soft cloth, and laid him in the manger. Mary and Joseph looked at the beautiful baby, and they looked at one another. They remembered the angel's promise to Mary. "Is it true he will be king of all his people?" they wondered. They reached out to gently caress the sleeping baby. "His name is Jesus," they whispered to each other.

Now on this same night, there were shepherds taking care of their flocks of sheep on a hillside above Bethlehem.

Suddenly a burst of light appeared on the hill in front of them. In the midst of the light stood an angel.

The shepherds drew back, hardly daring to look.

"Do not fear," said the angel. "I bring you marvelous good news. In Bethlehem, on this very night, a baby has been born. He is the Lord, the long-awaited Messiah."

"Where can we find him?" the astonished shepherds asked.

"Here is how you will know him," the angel said. "You will find a baby wrapped in swaddling clothes and lying in a manger."

Before the shepherds could recover from their surprise, the angel was joined by a whole chorus of angels, lighting up the night sky. "Glory to God in the highest, and on earth, peace!" the angels sang. Then, as quickly as they had come, the angels disappeared.

The shepherds turned to one another. "Did you see what I saw? Quick! Let's go and find this baby!" So, leaving their sheep, they hurried from the hillside and searched through the town until they found the stable.

They tiptoed in, past the cows and oxen and the dove and the dog and the scurrying mice. There, before their very eyes, a mother and father leaned over a tiny baby wrapped in swaddling clothes and lying in a manger.

For a while the shepherds watched, speechless. Then they left the stable and went into the streets. And they told everyone they met about the angel, the singing in the sky, and the beautiful baby they had found, just as the angel had promised.

When the shepherds had gone, Mary smiled at the baby Jesus in her arms. "Sleep, little one, sleep," she sang, and her heart overflowed with thankfulness to God.

Now also at this time, in a far country, there were wise men whose work it was to study the stars. They had heard that a new king would soon be born. One night while they were searching the heavens, the wise men saw a strange new star. "Might this star lead us to the child who is to be king?" one of the wise men said.

They decided to go and see. They got their camels ready. They wrapped their most precious gifts for the baby, and they set out on their long journey. And, lo and behold, after many weeks the shining star led them to Bethlehem and to the very place where the Baby Jesus and Mary and Joseph were.

The wise men were excited — and very tired — as they stepped down from their camels. "We've found the child!" they exclaimed. They bowed to Mary and Joseph. Then they knelt down in praise and adoration before this baby who would grow up to teach men and women and boys and girls how much God loves us, and how we are to love one another.

Then, "the presents!" one wise man said. "We mustn't forget the presents!" The wise men opened their treasure chests and gave the baby the gifts they had brought. There was shining gold; incense, which when burned makes a lovely smell; and myrrh, a kind of perfume.

And when they set the presents by little Jesus, he smiled.

The child Jesus grew.
And Mary and Joseph were filled with wonder and gratitude to God for all that had happened.